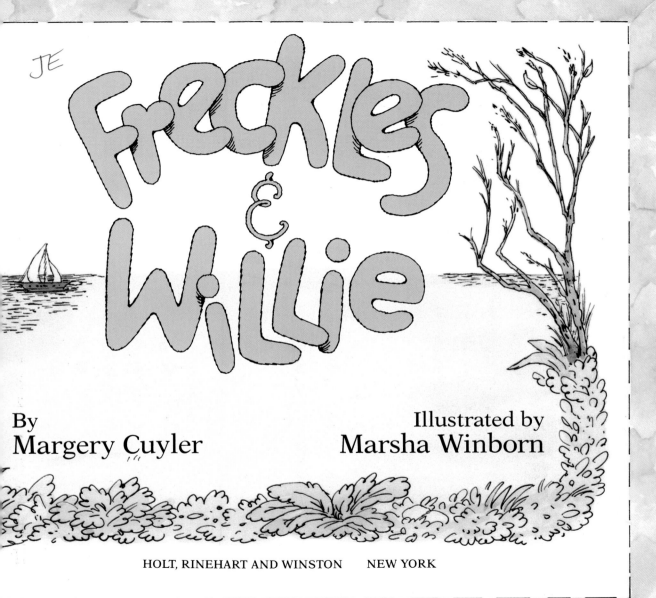

Freckles & Willie

By
Margery Cuyler

Illustrated by
Marsha Winborn

HOLT, RINEHART AND WINSTON   NEW YORK

Published by Holt, Rinehart and Winston,
383 Madison Avenue, New York, New York 10017.
Published simultaneously in Canada by Holt, Rinehart
and Winston of Canada, Limited.

Library of Congress Cataloging in Publication Data

Cuyler, Margery.
Freckles and Willie.

Summary: Freckles the dog is Willie's best friend until a little
girl who doesn't like dogs moves in across the street.
[1. Friendship—Fiction. 2. Dogs—Fiction. 3. Valentine's Day—
Fiction] I. Winborn, Marsha, ill. II. Title.
PZ7.C997Fr 1986   [E]   85–8646
ISBN: 0-03-003772-7

First Edition

Printed in Japan
1   3   5   7   9   10   8   6   4   2

ISBN 0-03-003772-7

For Sarah and Revel, with love

Freckles was Willie's best friend. He was always there when Willie needed him.

If Willie was lonely, Freckles would bring him something to play with.

If Willie was cold, Freckles would curl up on his feet like a warm pair of slippers.

If Willie was sad, Freckles would lean against him and make him feel better.

Because Willie was new in town, he had no other children to play with. So he always played with Freckles.

Early in February Willie woke up and looked at his calendar. Valentine's Day was less than two weeks away.

"I'll have to make a surprise valentine for Freckles," he said to himself. "It has to be perfect. It can't be too big or too small. And I'll draw dog biscuits around the edge."

Willie worked all day on the valentine. Finally it was finished, and he hid it in his closet.

Later that week another new family moved into a house across the street. A girl who was Willie's age came over to make friends.

"Hi," she said, "my name is Jane."

"I'm Willie," said Willie, "and this is Freckles."

Jane sneezed. "I'm allergic to dogs," she sniffed.

Willie patted Freckles and put him in the basement.

"You'll only have to stay here a few hours," he said.

Freckles began to bark.

While Willie and Jane played cards, Freckles barked louder.

"Does he always bark that loud?" Jane asked.

"No," said Willie. "He wants to be with us."

"I can't stand that noise," said Jane. "Let's go to my house to play."

So, for the next few days, Willie went to play at Jane's house. Freckles stayed home and waited for Willie to return.

When Willie walked in the door, Freckles wagged his tail.
"Jane says your tail looks like an old string," said Willie.

Freckles brought his favorite bone to Willie.
"Jane says that your bones smell," said Willie.

Freckles put his head on Willie's knee.
"I can't play with you right now," said Willie. "I have to make a valentine for Jane."

Freckles went down to the basement and lay on his pillow in the dark.

Willie worked hard on Jane's valentine. He made it out of red construction paper and aluminum foil. He pasted ribbons, lace, and stars on it.

On Valentine's Day, Willie left to take Jane's card next door. Freckles followed him outside.

"No, Freckles, you have to stay at home," said Willie. "Jane doesn't like dogs, remember?"

Freckles barely wagged his tail. He whimpered as Willie went over to Jane's house.

When Willie rang the doorbell, Jane answered the door.
"Hi," said Willie. "I brought you a present."

"Yuck!" she exclaimed. "You made me a valentine. I hate valentines." She slammed the door.

Willie blinked. His eyes filled with tears.
"I'm going home," he said.

When Willie got home, Freckles wasn't waiting for him.

"Freckles," called Willie. But Freckles didn't come.

Willie looked for Freckles in all of his favorite places. But Freckles wasn't in any of them. Not in the basement. Not in the kitchen. Not even under Willie's bed.

He looked for Freckles beneath the lilac bushes and in the garage.

"Freckles," he called, but Freckles still didn't come.

Suddenly, Willie remembered that he had made Freckles a valentine. He ran inside to get it. When he opened his closet door . . . there was Freckles.

"Freckles!" shouted Willie. "I've been looking all over for you. I thought you had run away."

Willie dragged Freckles out of the closet. He opened his arms, but Freckles didn't jump into them. He just lay down and put his head between his paws.

"Oh, Freckles," said Willie. "I'm sorry I was so mean." Freckles wagged his tail once.

"I'll never desert you again," said Willie.

Freckles wagged his tail harder.

Willie reached for Freckles' valentine.

"Look what I made for you!" he said. Willie tied the valentine to Freckles' collar. Freckles wagged his tail so hard, his whole body wiggled. He barked and barked.

"This valentine is for you because I love you," said Willie.

Freckles jumped up and licked Willie all over his face.

Later, while Willie did his homework, Freckles leaned against him. And when Willie went to sleep that night, Freckles curled up on his feet like a warm pair of slippers.